ORLANDO
The Marmalade Cat

A TRIP ABROAD
BY Kathleen Hale

Frederick Warne

FREDERICK WARNE

Published by the Penguin Group
Penguin Books Ltd, 27 Wrights Lane, London W8 5TZ, England
Penguin Books USA Inc., 375 Hudson Street, New York, N.Y. 10014, USA
Penguin Books Australia Ltd, Ringwood, Victoria, Australia
Penguin Books Canada Ltd, 10 Alcorn Avenue, Toronto, Ontario, Canada M4V 3B2
Penguin Books (N.Z.) Ltd, 182-190 Wairau Road, Auckland 10, New Zealand

Penguin Books Ltd, Registered Offices: Harmondsworth, Middlesex, England

First published 1939 by Country Life Ltd
This revised edition first published 1998 by Frederick Warne & Co.
10 9 8 7 6 5 4 3 2

ISBN 0 7232 4456 1

Printed and bound in Singapore by Imago Publishing

The illustrations in this book were originally drawn to plate by the author and lithographed by W. S. Cowell, Ipswich and London. For this edition the type has been reset and the illustrations scanned from a first edition.

O rlando and his kittens had all been "Tissiky" with bad colds.

"Sea-breezes blow away Sneezes," Orlando slyly suggested.

Their Master took the hint, said goodbye to Grace, Orlando's wife, who preferred to stay at home and put her feet up—packed the kittens in his pocket, Orlando in a basket and took them to Newhaven for a holiday by the sea. In the train Orlando in his basket was put in the guard's van.

During the journey, Orlando, full of curiosity, squeezed out of his basket to explore, and, when the train arrived, he jumped out to look for his family. But he couldn't find them on the platform, so he ran along to the quay to see if they were there.

On the quay he found all sorts of lovely things; a fish the fishing-smacks had left behind, and some milk that had leaked from a churn. He lapped it up, and this made him feel very cheerful.

He played with a clockwork mouse that a little boy had dropped, until he became sleepy; then he looked for a quiet place for a rest. Near some luggage he found a hot-water bottle, on which he had a snooze.

When he woke up he was surprised to see a snake which had travelled across the sea hidden in a crate of bananas. He told a docker, who said, "I'll give him to my Aunt Flossie, she dotes on serpents."

At that moment a crane lowered a tiger in a cage, out of the sky. "Fancy meeting you here!" smiled Orlando. The tiger, who was on his way with other animals to the zoo, purred with a foreign accent.

A Persian Prince with his Cat and all his wives had arrived by the same ship. Orlando bowed low and humbly because he knew that the smartest cats come from Persia.

Still looking for his family, Orlando followed some animals who were going with their owners up a gangway and found himself on board a ship going to France.

Suddenly a very loud siren was blown to show that the ship was ready to leave.

Orlando stopped up his ears and shut his eyes tight; when he opened them the sailors had taken the gangway down.

The engine started and slowly the quay with all its houses, stations, cranes and people waving goodbye, seemed to be sliding away. Orlando realised with dismay that he was separated from his family and was on his way to sea.

"Anyway I shall certainly lose my sneezes," sneezed Orlando.

A kind sailor called "Albair" fetched him a deck-chair and placed it where spray from the sea could not wet him and where he could hear the purring of the ship's engines, which reassured him.

"Are you interested in mice?" Albair asked, lending Orlando his Mickey Mouse weekly.

At lunch-time, Albair showed Orlando the way to the dining-saloon. He read the menu carefully, and asked for cold jellied soup, prawns and an "omelette surprise".

The prawns' whiskers gave him trouble, for they *would* get mixed up with his own, but the waiter helped to pick them off.

The omelette was very hot and folded round an ice-cream—that was the surprise part.

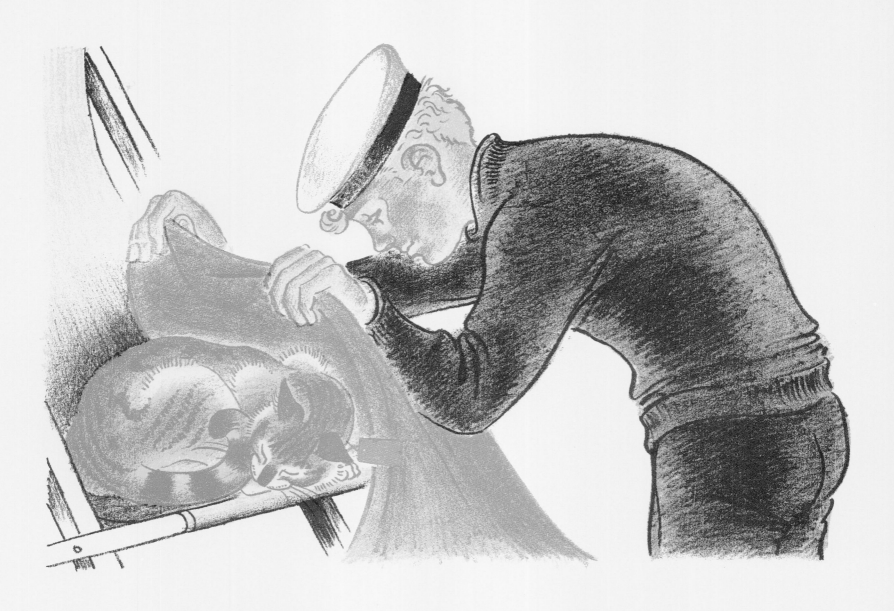

Albair took him back to his deck-chair, where he had "forty winks". He woke up later to find everyone walking about, twiddling the lenses of their field-glasses and saying, "I can see land!" Orlando climbed the rigging to get a better view; true enough, he could just see a long strip of coast.

The steamer glided into the harbour. The French quay with its houses, station, cranes, and people waving a welcome, seemed to be sliding towards them.

The porters were leaning on the railings sleepily watching the ship come in.

When the steamer was alongside the quay and the gangway had been let down the porters suddenly woke up and rushed on board shouting, "Porturr! Porturr!"

They sounded like unhappy seagulls in a storm, but they were really very pleased to have some work to do.

One of them seized Orlando's suitcase and as many others as he could grab, loaded himself up and then disappeared.

Wondering whether he would ever see his luggage again, Orlando followed the crowd to the Customs House.

There he found his porter very much out of breath, standing beside all the luggage spread out on two long tables.

A fussy little Customs Officer came along and told Orlando to open his case.

"Owch! And what may this be pray?" he asked, as something snapped his fingers.

"My mousetrap, Sir. I'm on holiday, you see," answered Orlando. "And now you've gone and lost the cheese!"

"Pardon, m'sieur," the officer said, and trotted off to tease someone else.

The porter led Orlando to the best seat he could find in the train.

He was lucky, it was a corner seat by the window. Then the porter mopped his brow with his handkerchief and said, "Oh la! la!" several times. "*Il fait chaud.*"

Orlando gave him a tip. He would spend it on a nice cool drink, or he might even take the money home to his family.

"Decent Cat, that," the porter told his friends.

Women were running up and down the platform selling peaches, and Orlando bought one with his last penny.

In this French port the train runs through the street for a short distance, and Orlando could see right into the shops in which people were buying their milk, fish and mousetraps.

The train passed so close to the cafés on the pavement that Orlando could almost have sipped the wine and coffee on the tables.

"Queer place this. Some of the shops sell 'Poisons'," said Orlando to himself.

The Guard shouted, "Paris next stop!"

"What! Paris!" said Orlando. "But I was going to Newhaven!" And he jumped out of the window.

Orlando found himself in front of a charming little hotel called the "Hotel of the Golden Cat", and as it was getting late he decided to stay the night. They gave him the best bedroom.

There was a telephone by the bed for him to order his breakfast by in the morning, and a tall French window. The wallpaper had fat blue birds printed on it, which reminded Orlando that he was hungry. He had a wash and a think, and then went out into the street again, wondering how to get back to Newhaven without any money for his fare.

BIÈRE 2
CAFÈ 1·50
VINS 2·0

It was now dark. Orlando heard gay music and laughter coming through a doorway. He went past an old lady who was adding up figures in a book, and found the sailors from the steamer sitting at little tables watching some lovely ladies dancing on a stage, to the music of a jazz band.

"Allo! Allo!" cried Albair to Orlando.

Orlando felt very shy, as all the ladies started calling him "Mini, Mini, Mini," which is the French for "puss, puss, puss," in high squeaky voices,

"What is this place?" he asked his friend. "A Café Concert, my little Cabbage," Albair answered, offering him a drink of milk.

After a drink his tummy was as tight as a drum, and he felt bolder.

The music excited Orlando so much that he jumped on to the stage and gave his world-famous imitation of a ham,

and then a dromedary.
He was a great success.

He called for a dish of snails for himself and Albair.

French people like eating cooked snails.

After Orlando had well licked the last snail shell, he danced with the prettiest lady, and they span round like tops to the music.

Albair passed his hat round and people threw money into it.

He gave it all to Orlando, who was extremely pleased, as he knew he could now pay his fare back to Newhaven.

All this excitement so long after his bedtime, made Orlando feel tired, and he decided to go back to his hotel. He bowed gracefully to the lady, patted Albair lovingly and said, "Goodnight All." They replied with a rousing cheer, and "Bonsoir Monsieur!"

He woke very late the next morning and telephoned for his breakfast.

When he had eaten it and had his bath he went to the quay to take a boat back to Newhaven. He was too late! It had sailed.

Orlando took a taxi to the nearest aerodrome, and climbed into a plane just leaving for England.

They were soon flying above the clouds which looked like a solid cotton-wool floor beneath them. This made Orlando feel safer. Now and again he could see the sea through it, and the ship he had missed, looking as small and neat as a little toy boat. The edge of England appeared.

"There's Newhaven!" said the Pilot.

Orlando quickly seized a parachute, ran along the wing and leapt off. It opened like an umbrella and he floated gently down.

He landed on the beach beside his Master, who was minding the kittens.
"Really!" exclaimed his Master. "Where *have* you been?"
"Oh la! la!" answered Orlando, fanning himself with a piece of seaweed.
All the people nudged each other and whispered, "That's a very French cat!"

The End